over, under & through

and other spatial concepts

by **tana hoban**

macmillan publishing company

new york

The photographs in this book were taken with two cameras: the Beseler Top-
con RE Super D (35mm) with 58mm and 135mm lenses, and the Hasselblad
500C (2¼″ x 2¼″) with Planar 80mm f2.8 lens. The films used were Plus-X
and Tri-X, developed in Ethol UFG and printed on Varigam paper in Dektol
developer.

for miela and bob

over

under

through

on

in

around

across

between

beside

below

against

behind